Cymbeline,
King of Britain

Sweet
Cherry

Published by Sweet Cherry Publishing Limited
Unit 36, Vulcan House,
Vulcan Road,
Leicester, LE5 3EF
United Kingdom

First published in the US in 2013
2020 hardback edition

2 4 6 8 10 9 7 5 3 1

ISBN: 978-1-78226-671-6

© Macaw Books

Cymbeline, King of Britain

Lexile® code numerical measure L = Lexile® 1110L

Cover design and illustrations by Macaw Books

www.sweetcherrypublishing.com

Printed and bound in India
I.TP002

About Shakespeare

William Shakespeare, regarded as the greatest writer in the English language, was born in Stratford-upon-Avon in Warwickshire, England, in 1564. He was the third of eight children born to John and Mary Shakespeare.

Shakespeare was a poet, playwright and dramatist. He is often known as England's national poet and the "Bard of Avon." Thirty-eight plays, one hundred and fifty-four sonnets, two long narrative poems and several other poems are attributed to him. Shakespeare's plays have been translated into every major existent language and are performed more often than those of any other playwright.

Cymbeline: He is the King of Britain and Imogen's father. He is a wise, gracious king. However, after the arrival of his new queen, he is led astray by her lies and wicked schemes.

Imogen: She is the daughter of King Cymbeline. She is beautiful, wise and quick-witted. Imogen marries the lowborn Posthumus against her father's wishes instead of Cloten, her father's stepson.

Iachimo: He is a clever, dishonest gentleman. He persuades Posthumus to enter into a wager with him, saying that he will be able to seduce his wife, Imogen. He resorts to trickery in order to succeed.

Posthumus: He was orphaned as a child and has been raised by King Cymbeline. He falls in love with Imogen, the king's daughter, and marries her in secret. He is banished by the king and later believes Iachimo's lie that his wife has been unfaithful.

Cymbeline, King of Britain

At about the same time as Augustus Caesar ruled over the Roman Empire, there lived in England a king called Cymbeline.

Cymbeline's first wife had died when his three children were

very young. He had two sons and
a daughter. However, tragedy
had struck in Cymbeline's life.
His daughter, Imogen, the eldest
of the three, grew up in her
father's court, but his two sons
were kept in the nursery and
had been kidnapped when they
were very young—the elder one
was around three years old and
the younger a mere infant. It

could never be ascertained what became of these two young boys.

Cymbeline had since married again. His second wife was a scheming witch, who treated Imogen cruelly. Though she hated Imogen, she often desired that Cymbeline's daughter be given in marriage to her son, Cloten, from a previous marriage. Her plan was simple.

In the event of Cymbeline's death, her son could be anointed the new King of England.

But Imogen realized what she was planning and therefore married quietly, without asking for the consent of her father or stepmother. Imogen's husband was Posthumus, one of the best scholars and most accomplished men of the times. His was a sad story, for his father had died before he was even born, in a war fighting for Cymbeline. His mother too had passed away shortly after his birth, unable to bear the grief of her husband's death.

He had been taken in by the great king himself and provided for ever since. Since his parents had died without giving him a name, Cymbeline named him Posthumus.

Imogen and Posthumus were taught by the same teachers

and had been very close since childhood. With the passing of time, their affection for each other blossomed into love, until such time as they decided to get married.

When the news reached the queen, who had employed several spies to keep tabs on her stepdaughter, she was extremely angry, for her evil designs on Cymbeline's throne had been thwarted. She at once went to inform the king about the marriage of his daughter. Needless to say, Cymbeline was furious upon learning this news, based on the fact that

his daughter had forgotten
the dignity of her birth and
married a common subject
at his court. He banished
Posthumus at once and the
poor scholar was forced to leave
his native country forever.

The queen then started
working on another plan to

meet her desires. She pretended to befriend Imogen and consoled her about the separation from her husband. She even went as far as to arrange a secret meeting between Posthumus and Imogen before the nobleman left for

Rome. She had decided that once Posthumus was gone, she would ask Imogen to marry her own son, Cloten, as her earlier marriage had been unlawful.

As the heartbroken pair bade farewell, Imogen gave her husband a diamond ring which had belonged to her mother as a

token to remember her by, and
he in turn placed a bracelet on
her wrist, which she promised
she would never take off.

Once Posthumus
arrived in Rome,
he met a group
of young men
who had come

from different parts of the world.
They talked about their own
loves and how the ladies from
their respective countries were
the most sought-after women
in the world. Posthumus,
remembering his fair wife,
recounted that there could never
be another woman like Imogen.

However, one man amongst those who had gathered there, called Iachimo, did not like what Posthumus said about Imogen, as he was sure that the ladies of Rome—his native country— were far superior to the women of Britain. Posthumus soon made a wager, whereby Iachimo would go to Britain and try to

woo Imogen. His task would
be to obtain the bracelet that
Posthumus had given Imogen,
and Posthumus would then give
him the ring Imogen had given
him before leaving. However,
if Iachimo did not succeed, he
would have to give Posthumus
a huge sum of money.

Iachimo was given a warm welcome by Imogen when she heard that he was a friend of her husband's. But when he tried to claim his love for her, Imogen started to ward him off. Iachimo realized that it would be nearly impossible to convince Imogen to give him the bracelet

as a token of
her love. He
also knew
that he would
stand to lose
a great deal if he
went back to Rome without
the bracelet. So he managed to

bribe Imogen's servants and hid himself in a trunk in her room.

That night, when Imogen finally fell asleep, Iachimo came out of hiding and started to make careful observations of the room. He even noted that Imogen had a small mole on her neck. Finally, he gently removed the bracelet from her wrist and was gone.

When he returned to Rome, Iachimo made a song and dance about the way in which Imogen had responded to his charms, and how he had even met her in her own room after everyone had retired for the night. He went on to give a rather lengthy

description of her room, all of which Posthumus knew to be true.

Finally, Iachimo revealed the bracelet that was the principal clause of the wager and showed it to Posthumus, also describing the mole Imogen had on her neck. Posthumus was completely heartbroken to hear all this and, with a heavy heart, he gave away the diamond ring that Imogen had given him when she bade him farewell.

Iachimo had successfully proved to Posthumus that Imogen's love for him was truly false.

Unable to calm his jealous rage against Imogen, Posthumus wrote to his friend Pisanio in Britain, who was an old friend of theirs. He recounted the tale of Imogen's betrayal, and asked him to take her to Milford-Haven—a seaport in Wales—

and kill her. He wrote another
letter to Imogen, declaring that
his love for her was so great
that he was returning to see
her again at Milford-Haven,
braving her father's orders against
him. Imogen, on receiving the
letter, unsuspectingly left for
the seaport with Pisanio.

But Pisanio, though loyal to
Posthumus, could not bring himself
to carry out this shameful deed
and told Imogen of her husband's
orders. Imogen was completely
crestfallen. Pisanio comforted her
and told her of his plan to make
Posthumus pay for his actions.
He convinced her to dress up like

a man and then travel to Rome to confront her husband.

Pisanio had to return to court before he was missed. But before leaving, he gave Imogen a vial containing a special liquid given to him by the queen. Little did he know that the queen, hating his closeness to both Imogen and Posthumus, had given him a vial of poison, telling him that it was a special medicine that could cure any affliction. But the physician from whom she had acquired it, knowing of the queen's evil ways, had made some changes to the composition. The liquid would put the person into a deep sleep, making everyone think that he or she was dead. Only later, when the potency wore off, would the person wake from their deep slumber.

Imogen soon set off for
Rome with this special tonic.
But destiny had other plans for
her. She lost her way and ended
up at the home of her brothers,
who had been kidnapped.
They had been taken by a man
called Bellarius, a lord at the
court of Cymbeline. He had

been falsely accused of treason and, as revenge, had stolen the infant princes. But hidden away in his cave, he had grown fond of them and raised them as his own children. It was now time for them to join the army.

Imogen, lost in the forest, had stumbled upon their cave, hungry and cold. Unable to continue any farther, she stopped there to rest. Bellarius and her two brothers found her and took her in. They offered her food,

but when she tried to give them
money for it, the noblemen
refused. They asked her where
she was going and what her name
was. Remember, all this time
they thought Imogen was a man.

Imogen replied that her
name was Fidele and that she
was bound for Italy, but the
bad weather had made her lose

her way. Bellarius immediately
invited Fidele to come inside
and share the venison they had
brought back from their hunt.
Fidele, it turned out, was an
excellent cook and was soon
able to charm his way into
the hearts of the three men.

After a while, Imogen,
who had grown to love the two
boys like her own brothers, not
knowing their true identity, told
them that she was
well rested and it
was time for her
was time for her
to continue her
journey to Italy

from Milford-Haven. Though she would have loved to stay on with them, she still had to confront Posthumus over his evil actions.

But alas, she started to feel a little unwell. The boys told her to rest while they went into the forest and brought back some more food. No sooner did Bellarius and the

boys leave than Imogen took
a sip of the curing liquid that
Pisanio had given her. Within
a few minutes, she was sleeping
in a death-like slumber.

When the men
returned, Imogen's
brother Polydore
was the first to
enter the cave and

find Fidele dead. He was very
sad, and behaved as if he had
known Fidele for a long time.
Bellarius, who had also grown
fond of the young boy, decided
to carry their guest to the
forest and bury him there.

But as the men left her in
the forest and returned to their
cave, the drug wore off and

Imogen woke up. She wondered how she had come to be covered in flowers, in the middle of the forest. She realized that perhaps she had dreamed the whole thing and set off immediately towards Milford-Haven. She had decided she would seek out her husband like as a page and take up the matter with him.

But little did Imogen know of the developments that had taken place while she was away from the palace. Augustus Caesar, the supreme leader of Rome, had declared war on Cymbeline of Britain and a large Roman army had already landed

in Britain. Posthumus
was part of that army.

But Posthumus was
not the same man who
had ordered his wife to
be killed. He had come
back with the Roman
army not to fight for
them, but against them.
He still believed that
his wife had been cruel
to him, but news of her
death following a letter
from Pisanio weighed
heavily on his mind. He
decided that he would
fight the war, and either
get killed fighting or

be executed by Cymbeline for coming back to the country.

Before Imogen could reach the seaport, she was captured

by the Roman army and appointed as a page to Lucius, the valiant Roman general. Unknown to her, her brothers Polydore and Cadwal had joined the British army along with their father, Bellarius, who had long repented for the injury he had caused Cymbeline by kidnapping his sons.

Finally, when the two armies fought, the British forces surely would have been defeated had it not been for the bravery displayed by Posthumus, Bellarius and the two brothers, who managed

to save the king and let the
battle be won in Britain's
favor. Posthumus did not die
fighting and handed himself
over to one of Cymbeline's
officers, agreeing to die for
having disobeyed the king's
orders and having come back
to Britain against his wishes.

Imogen and her general had
been captured and presented
before Cymbeline, as had
Iachimo, the villain who now
served as a commander in the
Roman army. Posthumus too
had been brought to court to
be punished for returning. The
noble Bellarius and his two sons

were also present, for they were to be rewarded for their gallantry.

Lucius, the Roman general, was the first to speak. He said that while he would gladly embrace death at the hands of his enemies, he begged that Imogen, or Fidele as he called him, be spared. He was after all a British national and was a good page. He begged Cymbeline to spare him, even if he spared no one else.

Cymbeline had not been able to recognize his own daughter because she was dressed in male clothes, but he felt that there was some connection between him and this noble page. So he forgave Imogen at once

and agreed to give her anything she desired. Everyone turned to look at the page to see what she would request from the king.

But all that she wanted to know
was how Iachimo had found the
ring that he now wore on his
finger, the same ring that she had
given to Posthumus.

Cymbeline was
only too glad to
grant her this wish
and threatened

Iachimo with torture if he did
not confess. Iachimo, who was
already scared in the presence of
the king, told them everything,
from accepting the wager
from Posthumus to deceiving
Imogen and Posthumus. When
Posthumus heard this news he
was completely shattered. He

immediately confessed his crime before the king and wept profusely.

Imogen now understood her husband's actions and forgave him. She realized that he too had been deceived. She immediately revealed herself to the people and the court, and Cymbeline was beside himself with joy for having finally found his daughter again. He was so happy that not only did he pardon Posthumus, but he even acknowledged

their wedding and accepted
him as his son-in-law.

Bellarius chose this joyous
moment to confess about his
sons and presented the king's
own long-lost sons before him.
Obviously the king did not
consider punishing Bellarius,
because he had brought only

joy to him that day. Now that
everything had been resolved,
Imogen asked her father
to also forgive the Roman
general Lucius, and
with his help,
Britain and Rome
signed a successful
peace treaty.

Everyone was finally happy with the way things had turned out.

The evil queen, though, died from depression since none of her plans had succeeded!